A Bird in a Box

By Cecilia Minden

Pam has a pet shop.

Pam sells pets.

"Do you have birds?"

"Yes, I have birds."

"Do you have blue birds?"

"Yes, I have blue birds."

"I like blue birds."

"I like blue birds that sing."

 "I have a blue bird that sings."

"I have a blue bird just for you."

12 Pam puts the blue bird in a box.

"I like this blue bird just for me."

Word List

sight words

a	blue	have	me	you
bird	Do	I	sing	
birds	for	like	sings	

short a words	short e words	short i words	short o words	short u words
has	pet	in	box	just
Pam	pets	this	shop	puts
that	sells			
	Yes			

Pam has a pet shop.
Pam sells pets.
"Do you have birds?"
"Yes, I have birds."
"Do you have blue birds?"
"Yes, I have blue birds."
"I like blue birds."
"I like blue birds that sing."
"I have a blue bird that sings."
"I have a blue bird just for you."
Pam puts the blue bird in a box.
"I like this blue bird just for me."

CHERRY BLOSSOM PRESS

Published in the United States of America by Cherry Lake Publishing Group
Ann Arbor, Michigan
www.cherrylakepublishing.com

Illustrator: Kelsey Collings
Book Designer: Melinda Millward

Cherry Blossom Press is an imprint of Cherry Lake Publishing Group.

Library of Congress Cataloging-in-Publication Data

Names: Minden, Cecilia, author. | Collings, Kelsey, illustrator.
Title: A bird in a box / by Cecilia Minden ; illustrated by Kelsey Collings.
Description: Ann Arbor, Michigan : Cherry Lake Publishing, 2021. | Series: Little blossom stories
Identifiers: LCCN 2021007803 (print) | LCCN 2021007804 (ebook) | ISBN 9781534188037
   (paperback) | ISBN 9781534189430 (pdf) | ISBN 9781534190832 (ebook)
Subjects: LCSH: Readers (Primary)
Classification: LCC PE1119.2 .M5632 2021 (print) | LCC PE1119.2 (ebook) | DDC 428.6/2—dc23
LC record available at https://lccn.loc.gov/2021007803
LC ebook record available at https://lccn.loc.gov/2021007804

Cherry Lake Publishing Group would like to acknowledge the work of the Partnership for 21st Century Learning, a Network of Battelle for Kids. Please visit http://www.battelleforkids.org/networks/p21 for more information.

Printed in the United States of America
Corporate Graphics

Cecilia Minden is the former director of the Language and Literacy Program at Harvard Graduate School of Education. She earned her PhD in Reading Education at the University of Virginia. Dr. Minden has written extensively for early readers. She is passionate about matching children to the very book they need to improve their skills and progress to a deeper understanding of all the wonder books can hold. Dr. Minden and her family live in McKinney, Texas.